T·H·E
GROWING-UP
FEET

Beverly Cleary

ILLUSTRATED BY
DyAnne DiSalvo-Ryan

A Young Yearling Special

Published by
Dell Publishing
a division of
The Bantam Doubleday Dell Publishing Group, Inc.
666 Fifth Avenue
New York, New York 10103

The trademark Yearling® is registered in the U.S. Patent and
Trademark Office.

ISBN: 0-440-40109-7

Reprinted by arrangement with William Morrow and Company, Inc.

Printed in the United States of America

November 1988

10 9 8 7 6 5 4 3

W A K

"When are my feet going to grow up?" Jimmy
asked one morning as he wiggled his toes.

"They're growing all the time," said Mother.
"They have grown so much that it is time to go to
the shoe store and talk to Mr. Markle about new
shoes."

"For me, too?" asked Janet, Jimmy's twin sister.

"For both of you," said Mother.

"Our feet are growing up!" shouted Jimmy. "Our feet are growing up!"

"New shoes, new shoes, we're going to get new shoes!" sang Janet. Then she said, "And I'm going to surprise Mr. Lemon with new shoes when he brings the mail." Janet liked to surprise people, especially Mr. Lemon.

Mother and the twins drove to the shoe store, where they sat in three chairs in a row, with Mother in the middle.

Mr. Markle pulled up a stool and sat down in front of them. "What will my favorite customers have today?" he asked.

"Shoes," said Jimmy. "Our feet are growing up."

"No kidding," said Mr. Markle. He felt the toes of Jimmy's and Janet's shoes. Then he took off their shoes and asked each of them to stand on his measuring stick while he slid the wooden piece to the tips of their toes.

Mr. Markle shook his head. "Sorry," he said.
"You kids aren't ready for new shoes."

No new shoes! Jimmy and Janet looked at
Mother and said, "You told us we were ready for
new shoes."

Mother sighed. "Mothers can be wrong sometimes," she said. That made Jimmy and Janet feel better—a little, but not much.

Mr. Markle looked disappointed, too. He sniffed and rubbed his eyes with his fists and looked so silly that Jimmy and Janet almost smiled.

Janet leaned against Mother. "I won't have a
surprise for Mr. Lemon today," she said and looked
very, very sad. "Mr. Lemon likes me to surprise him."
"We'll think of another surprise," said Mother.
"But it won't be new shoes," answered Janet.

"I *want* new shoes," said Jimmy.

"Now, Jimmy," said Mother. "You're a big boy."

"No, I'm not!" said Jimmy. "My feet didn't grow up."

"How would you each like a balloon?" asked Mr. Markle.

Jimmy and Janet took the balloons, but they did not really want balloons. They wanted new shoes.

"You know something?" said Mr. Markle. "We have some boots on sale."

"We can't buy boots to fit old shoes," said Mother.

"These boots stretch," said Mr. Markle. "They will fit old shoes and new shoes, too. And you know something else? These boots are red."

Red boots. Jimmy and Janet looked up at Mother.
"Good," said Mother. "Let's buy new boots."
"For me?" asked Jimmy.
"For me?" asked Janet.
"For both of you," said Mother.

Mr. Markle brought out bright red boots, which fit the old shoes. "There you are, kids," he said. "Just what the Easter Bunny ordered."

Jimmy and Janet thought Mr. Markle was such a silly man. They knew Easter was a long time ago.

Jimmy wore his boots, but Janet carried hers in
their box. The twins were so happy they didn't even
stop to pet the hobby horse on their way out the door.
Mother remembered to say "Thank you" to Mr. Markle.

When Mother and the twins returned home,
they found Mr. Lemon had already delivered the
mail. Janet hid her box of boots in the closet. "I'm
going to save my boots to show Daddy," she said,
"and tomorrow I will surprise Mr. Lemon."

"Jimmy, don't you want to take off your boots?" asked Mother.

"No," said Jimmy and ran out into the yard. In a little while he came back. "I can't find any puddles," he said.

"Of course there aren't any puddles," said
Mother. "It isn't raining."

"When is it going to rain?" asked Jimmy.

"I don't know," answered Mother. "There aren't
any clouds, so it won't rain today."

"Will it rain tomorrow?" asked Jimmy.

"I don't know," said Mother. "I don't think so."

"The next day?" asked Jimmy.

"I don't know." Mother sounded tired as she made sandwiches for lunch.

New boots and no puddles. Jimmy pretended he
was walking in puddles, but he wanted *real* puddles
with *real* water. Janet waited and waited for Daddy
to come home so she could show him her red
boots in their box.

When Daddy came home he was surprised once
to see Jimmy wearing new boots and surprised
twice when Janet opened her box to show him
her boots. After the surprise, Janet put her boots
on, too.

"Our feet didn't grow up," said Jimmy, "and
Mother said they did."
"Don't worry. They will," said Daddy.

Jimmy and Janet wore their boots while they ate their dinner. Their feet were hot, but they didn't care. At bedtime they pulled their boots on over the feet of their sleepers.

When Mother said they could not sleep with boots over their sleepers because their feet would be too hot, they slept with their boots on their hands.

In the morning Jimmy and Janet pulled their
new boots on over their old shoes. "My
goodness," said Mother. "You will wear your
boots out before we have any rain."

This morning Daddy put on an old pair of pants and a sweatshirt.

"Are you going to stay home today?" asked Jimmy as he watched Daddy shave. He liked to watch so he would know how when he was old enough to shave off whiskers of his own.

"Yes. Today is Saturday," answered Daddy.

Janet, who knew she would never have whiskers
like Daddy, was in the kitchen with Mother. "I
wish Mr. Lemon would hurry up and come," she
said.

After breakfast Jimmy said to Daddy, "If we
went for a walk, maybe we could find some puddles."
Daddy smiled. "I'm afraid not, but I know what
we can do. Come outside with me."
"I'm going to sit on the front step and watch for
Mr. Lemon," said Janet.

Daddy backed the car out of the garage. Then he turned on the hose and started to wash the car. Water ran down the driveway. "Puddles!" shouted Jimmy and began to splash. Janet decided Mr. Lemon would be surprised to see wet boots when the sun was shining, so she splashed, too.

Mother stood in the doorway watching her
twins have fun. Daddy turned the hose on the
grass and made a big puddle. Jimmy and Janet
squished and splashed in the wet grass. Their
boots were wet, but their shoes were dry.

Then they saw Mr. Lemon coming down the street with his leather bag full of letters and catalogs. "You stay here," Janet told Jimmy. "I want to surprise Mr. Lemon."

"Okay," said Jimmy and went on stomping and splashing.

"Say!" said Mr. Lemon when Janet ran to meet him. "Look at those red boots and all those wet footprints when the sun is shining." Janet was happy because she could see Mr. Lemon was really surprised.

When the mailman reached the sidewalk, Jimmy stopped splashing to explain, "My feet didn't grow up. They are still the same size inside my boots."

"Don't worry," said Mr. Lemon. "Before you know it, your feet will be bigger than mine."

"They will?" Jimmy looked at Mr. Lemon's feet. They were even bigger than Daddy's feet.

"And do you know something?" asked Mr. Lemon as he handed Jimmy the catalogs to carry. "When you get new shoes, those boots will grow to fit."

Now it was Janet's turn to be surprised. "How did you know?" she asked Mr. Lemon.

"I've learned a thing or two in my lifetime," said Mr. Lemon.

Jimmy and Janet splashed in their puddle. "We have growing-up feet!" they shouted. "We have growing-up boots, too!"

Mr. Lemon said so, and he knew a thing or two.